Esther Miskotte

DRAGONS DON'T
EAT VEGETABLES!

Clavis

NEW YORK

One beautiful day Bear and Ralphie were enjoying
a basket filled with blackberries and apples.
Just as Bear said, "Yummy, these are delicious!"
a shadow passed over the woods
as if a dark cloud had passed in front of the sun.

First published in Belgium and Holland by Clavis Uitgeverij, Hasselt – Amsterdam, 2014
Copyright © 2014, Clavis Uitgeverij

English translation from the Dutch by Clavis Publishing Inc. New York
Copyright © 2015 for the English language edition: Clavis Publishing Inc. New York

Visit us on the web at www.clavisbooks.com

Dragons Don't Eat Vegetables! written and illustrated by Esther Miskotte
Original title: *Drakensnot*
Translated from the Dutch by Clavis Publishing

ISBN 978-1-60537-239-6

This book was printed in September 2015 at Publikum d.o.o., Slavka Rodica 6, Belgrade, Serbia

First Edition
10 9 8 7 6 5 4 3 2 1

Clavis Publishing supports the First Amendment and celebrates the right to read

Suddenly there was a huge thud.
The trees shook.
"What was that?" Ralphie yelled.
"It came from the hill," Bear replied.
"Come on, let's go take a look!"

Other animals heard the crash too.
They followed Bear and Ralphie.
It was getting misty and the woods looked sad.
The birds had stopped singing.
Even the flowers were drooping.

The animals reached the foot of the hill.
"I can't see a thing!" the hedgehog squealed.
"Ssh!" Bear whispered.
"I hear something. Listen."
A strange rumbling noise was coming
from the top of the hill.

Could it be thunder?
"I'll go first," Ralphie said.
The animals followed him.
They were panting
as they reached the top of the hill.

Suddenly…

"WAAAAAACHOOOOOO!"

A huge sneeze blew the mist apart.

"AAAAAACHOOOOO!"

"Look out! A monster!"

The animals tumbled down the hill
and scurried back into the woods as fast as they could.

It was quiet on the hill.

But where was Ralphie?

Oh no, Ralphie was still on the hill!

"Hello," Ralphie squeaked,
"Nice to meet you. I am Ralphie Rabbit."
"I'm Django," the monster growled. "Django the dragon."
"Oh, we don't see many dragons here in our woods…."
"Of course not!" Django said. "Dragons don't like woods.
All those trees. YUCK! I was on my way to the mountains.
But my nose is all stuffed up so I had to make
an emergency landing."

"Ah," Ralphie smiled, "so you won't be staying long then…."
"I can't fly until I get better," Django grumbled.
"And that could take a week. AAAA…AAAA…."
Before the dragon could go CHOOOO!
Ralphie was running down the hill.

"A week?!" the hedgehog squeaked.
"He'll be staying for a week?
But his stinky breath is making all the trees die!"
"Can you scare him off?" the mouse asked Bear.
Bear shook his head. "If he gets hungry,
that dragon could eat me in one bite!
And he'd have you guys for dessert."
The animals looked at each other with big eyes.
Now what?
They thought hard.
"Of course!" Ralphie said suddenly.
"We just have to make sure he doesn't get hungry.
I'll be right back!"
"Wait! Are you crazy?" Bear shouted.
But Ralphie had already left.
And he'd taken the apples with him.

"Hi, Mister Django," Ralphie said.
"These are for you!"
"What's that?" the dragon growled.
"Apples. They're very healthy!"

"Dragons don't eat apples,
dragons eat princesses!"
Django snarled.
"And buffaloes and sausages
and steak! Do you have steak?"
"Eat the apples," Ralphie said.
"They'll help make you better."

"Do you think so?
Okay, I'll give it a try!"
Django took a huge bite.
"Nooo!" Ralphie screamed.
"Not the basket!"

"Sorry!" Django said.
Then his face changed.
"Yum! Those apple things
are delicious!
Do you have any more?"

Then the animals got busy!
They gathered vegetables and fruit and herbs.
They got wood and kitchenware….
All day long they ran up and down the hill.

That night Ralphie introduced his friends to the dragon.
"Aren't you afraid?" Django rumbled, surprised.
"Oh no," Bear said. "Please blow a flame so we can start to cook!"

"Cook? What are you making?" Django asked.
"We're making vegetable soup," Ralphie said proudly.
"Vegetable soup?! YECH!" Django rumbled.
"Dragons don't eat vegetables!"
But the soup smelled good – and the
dragon was getting hungry.

Each of the animals got a bowl.
Django slurped from the pot.
Then he licked it clean.
"That was good! Do you have more?"

The next day Ralphie brought
Django a breakfast of fruit.
The dragon growled, but ate everything.
"Yummy!" he said.
Then, "Do you have more?"

There was cucumber salad for lunch.
"Yummy!" the dragon said.
"Do you have more?"

For dinner the animals
made pumpkin soup.
"Yummy!" Django said.
"Do you have more?!"

"Do you have more of those?"
Django asked after a pile
of cherries.

"Do you have more of these?"
after a dish of mushrooms.

Django ate everything and always asked for more.
"Did you guys notice that I stopped sneezing?"
Django said on the third day. "I feel great!
Do you think it could be all the vegetables?"

That night Ralphie kept the dragon company on the hill.
When the fire went out, they looked at the stars.
Django told exciting stories from his dragon life.

Then Ralphie sang songs
until the dragon fell asleep.

The next morning Django looked glorious.
He was bright green and his wings were shining.
"My little friends," he said,
"you took great care of me!
I had a wonderful time here,
but now I really should be going."
He roared and ran and lifted into the sky
as if he were light as a feather.
The animals watched him as he flew away.
"He ended up being pretty nice…." Ralphie said with a sigh.
The sky was clear and the sun was shining.

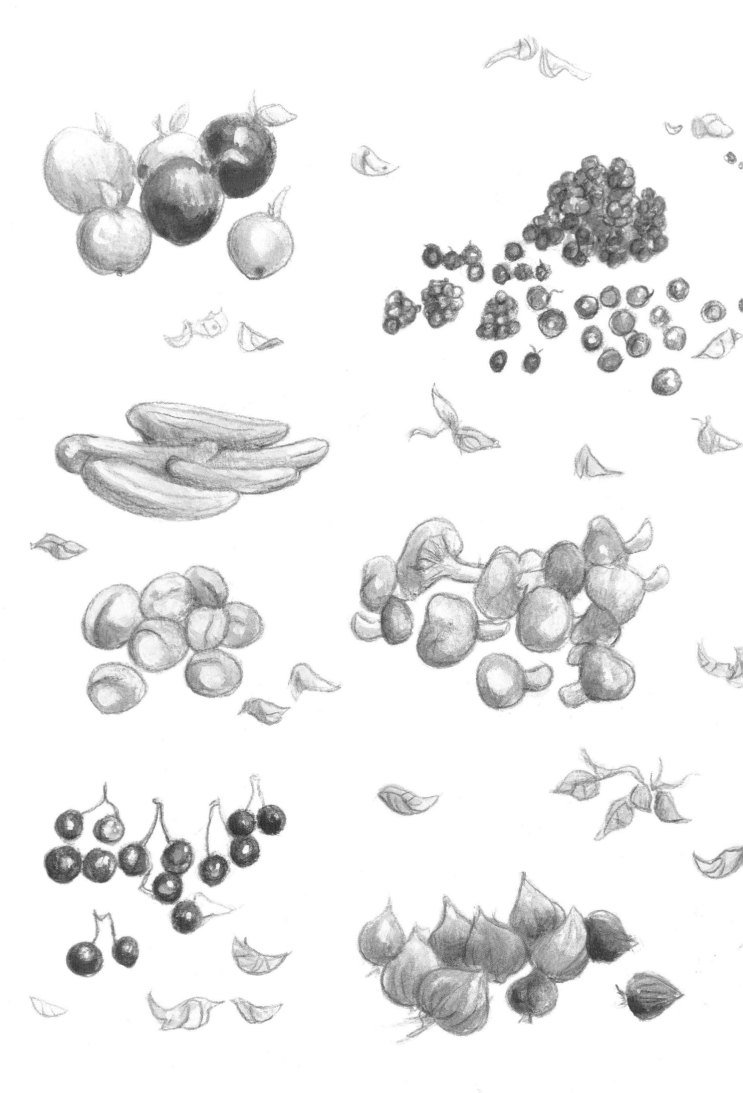